This book belongs to:

_____

_____

_____

First published 2017 by Walker Books Ltd
87 Vauxhall Walk, London SE11 5HJ

This edition published 2018

2 4 6 8 10 9 7 5 3 1

© 1990–2018 Lucy Cousins
Lucy Cousins font © 1990–2018 Lucy Cousins

The author/illustrator has asserted her moral rights

Maisy™. Maisy is a trademark of Walker Books Ltd, London

Printed in China

British Library Cataloguing in Publication Data:
a catalogue record for this book is
available from the British Library.

ISBN 978-1-4063-7707-1

www.walker.co.uk

Maisy Goes to the Bookshop

Lucy Cousins

WALKER BOOKS
AND SUBSIDIARIES
LONDON • BOSTON • SYDNEY • AUCKLAND

Today Maisy is going to the bookshop. She wants to buy a new book.

We Love Books

Wow! The shelves are full of so many books!

Which one will Maisy
like the most?

She reads
a big brown
book about
bears...

one long blue
book about
fish...

a noisy
book about
trucks ...

Brrm,
brrm!

and a book about
things to draw and
paint. It's the best!

Ostrich, the shopkeeper, helps Maisy find a beautiful book about birds. She can't wait to read it with her friend Tallulah!

What a surprise! Charley jumps
out from behind the shelves.
"Ahoy, Maisy!" he says.

"I'm reading a book about pirates.
I can imagine **US** as pirates!"

Next they meet Cyril.
"One day I want to be a cowboy
or an astronaut! Look at this
amazing rocket!"

Hello Eddie! What are you reading about?

It's story time! Hooray! Ostrich reads a book about a dinosaur.

Then Maisy and friends share
their favourite books.

Now everyone is feeling hungry.
The food at the café is so yummy!

Maisy pays for her books at the till and gets a receipt. "Thank you, Ostrich!" she says.

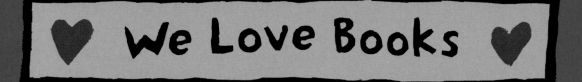

Bye Eddie! Bye Charley! Bye Cyril!
It's time for Maisy to get
the bus to Tallulah's house.

Maisy tells Tallulah about her wonderful day at the bookshop. She loves her present!

Then they read Tallulah's new book together. Over and over again ... and out LOUD!